THIS CANDLEWICK BOOK BELONGS TO:

_____

_____

_____

Michael Rosen's SAD BOOK

words by
Michael Rosen

pictures by
Quentin Blake

CANDLEWICK PRESS
CAMBRIDGE, MASSACHUSETTS

This is me being sad.
Maybe you think I'm happy in this picture.
Really I'm sad but pretending I'm happy.
I'm doing that because I think people won't
like me if I look sad.

Sometimes sad is very big.
It's everywhere. All over me.

Then I look like this.
And there's nothing I can do about it.

What makes me most sad is when I think
about my son Eddie. He died. I loved him
very, very much but he died anyway.

Sometimes this makes me really angry.
I say to myself, "How dare he go and die like that?
How dare he make me sad."

Eddie doesn't say anything,
because he's not here anymore.

Sometimes I want to talk about all this to someone.
Like my mum. But she's not here anymore, either. So I can't.
I find someone else. And I tell them all about it.

Sometimes I don't want to talk about it.
Not to anyone. No one. No one at all.
I just want to think about it on my own.
Because it's mine. And no one else's.

Sometimes because I'm sad I do crazy things—like shouting in the shower . . .

banging a spoon on the table . . .

or making my cheeks go *whooph, boooph, whooph.*

Sometimes because I'm sad I do bad things.
I can't tell you what they are.
They're too bad. And it's not fair to the cat.

Sometimes I'm sad and I don't know why.
It's just a cloud that comes along and covers me up.
It's not because Eddie's gone.
It's not because my mum's gone. It's just because.

Maybe it's because things now aren't like they were a few years ago.
Like my family. It's not the same as it was a few years ago.
So what happens is that there's a sad place inside me
because things aren't the same.

I've been trying to figure out ways of being sad that
don't hurt so much. Here are some of them:

I tell myself that everyone has sad stuff.
I'm not the only one. Maybe you have some too.

Every day I try to do one thing I can be proud of.
Then, when I go to bed, I think very, very, very
hard about this one thing.

I tell myself that being sad isn't the same
as being horrible. I'm sad, not bad.

Every day I try to do one thing that means
I have a good time. It can be anything so long
as it doesn't make anyone else unhappy.

And sometimes I write about sad.

Where is sad?
Sad is anywhere.
It comes along and finds you.

When is sad?
Sad is any time.
It comes along and finds you.

Who is sad?
Sad is anyone.
It comes along and finds you.

I write:

Sad is a place
that is deep and dark
like the space
under the bed

Sad is a place
that is high and light
like the sky
above my head

When it's deep and dark
I don't dare go there

When it's high and light
I want to be thin air.

This last bit means that I don't want to be here.
I just want to disappear.

But sometimes I find myself looking at things:
faces at a window . . .

a crane and a train full of people going past.

And then I remember things.
My mum in the rain.

Eddie walking along the street,
laughing and laughing and laughing.

Doing his old-man act in the school play.

The two of us playing catch on and off the sofa.

And birthdays . . . I love birthdays.

Not just mine—other people's as well.

Happy birthday to you . . . and all that.

And candles.

There must be candles.

First U.S. paperback edition 2008

The Library of Congress has cataloged the hardcover edition as follows:

Rosen, Michael, date.
Michael Rosen's sad book / words by Michael Rosen ; pictures by Quentin Blake. —1st U.S. ed.
p.   cm.
Summary: A man tells about all the emotions that accompany
his sadness over the death of his son, and how he tries to cope.
ISBN 978-0-7636-2597-9 (hardcover)
[1. Sadness—Fiction. 2. Emotions—Fiction.]
I. Title: Sad book. II. Blake, Quentin, ill. III. Title.
PZ7.R71867Mg 2005
[E]—dc22   2004045787

ISBN 978-0-7636-4104-7 (paperback)

2 4 6 8 10 9 7 5 3 1

Printed in China

This book was typeset in Bookman.
The illustrations were done in watercolor and ink.

Candlewick Press
2067 Massachusetts Avenue
Cambridge, Massachusetts 02140

visit us at www.candlewick.com

Michael Rosen is an award-winning author and anthologist of books for young readers, including *Shakespeare's Romeo and Juliet*, illustrated by Jane Ray, and *Shakespeare: His Work and His World*, illustrated by Robert Ingpen, which was a *School Library Journal* Best Book of the Year and a New York Public Library 100 Titles for Reading and Sharing selection. In 1997 he received the Eleanor Farjeon Award for service to children's literature. Michael Rosen lives in London.

Quentin Blake has illustrated more than 250 books by many writers, notably John Yeoman, Russell Hoban, Joan Aiken, Michael Rosen, and, most famously, Roald Dahl. He is also well known for his own picture books, such as *Clown* and *Zagazoo*. Quentin Blake was a tutor at the Royal College of Art from 1965 to 1988, and for eight of those years was head of the Illustration Department. In 1999 he was appointed the first British Children's Laureate, and in 2002 the Quentin Blake Europe School in Berlin was named for him. He is also a recipient of the Hans Christian Andersen Award for Illustration. Quentin Blake lives in London.